D1487717

Tabitha Tabby's Fantastic Flavor

by Jean Lewis
illustrated by Pam Peltier

A GOLDEN BOOK · NEW YORK
Western Publishing Company, Inc., Racine, Wisconsin 53404

Father Tabby bustled into the bright, shiny kitchen of Tabby's Ice-Cream Shop. "Tabitha!" he scolded. "You're supposed to clean the ice-cream maker, not play with it."

"But, Papa, I did clean it," answered Tabitha. "Now I'm making ice cream, just for fun."

Father Tabby made a face.

"See, Papa, I mixed the leftover vanilla, chocolate, and strawberry ice cream with marshmallow fudge syrup. I put in nuts, raisins, cherries, half a banana, and a squirt of lemon fizz. I mixed it all up in the blender, just the way I've seen you do, Papa. And then I poured it into the ice-cream maker. It should be just about ready."

Tabitha scooped out a little of the ice cream into a cup.

"Taste it, Papa," begged Tabitha. "Please."

"Oh, all right," said Father. "Just for you, Tabitha. Mmm," he said, licking his whiskers.

Just then Mother Tabby came in, and she took a taste. "Mm-mm," said Mother, licking her whiskers, too.

Tabitha's younger brother Tom appeared, and he took a taste. "Wow!" he said, reaching for more.

"Tabitha," said Father, "you have just invented a fantastic new flavor of ice cream."

"What shall we call it?" asked Mother.

"How about Tabitha Tabby's Fantastic Flavor?" suggested Tom.

"Perfect," said Father, and he proudly added it to Tabby's list of ice creams.

"By the way, Tabitha, you had better write down the recipe," said Father.

"Oh, don't worry," Tabitha answered. "I'll remember it in my head."

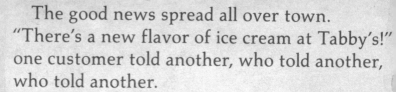

The good news spread all over town.
"There's a new flavor of ice cream at Tabby's!"
one customer told another, who told another,
who told another.

Soon they were lining up for sodas, sundaes,
shakes, splits, and double dips all made with
T.T.F.F.—Tabitha Tabby's Fantastic Flavor.

Then the big ice-cream companies heard
about it. Each company wanted to buy Tabitha's
recipe. Each one wanted to make her rich, they
said. But her answer was always the same.

"No, T.T.F.F. belongs to the Tabby family.
And Tabby's is the only place to buy it!"

Tabitha never wrote the recipe down. She
kept it in her head. It was her secret.

Years went by, and Father Tabby had long since retired. Tabitha ran the shop with Tom and his wife and some of their grandchildren. And T.T.F.F. was still the most popular ice cream in town.

Then one day something happened to change that. The New-Vel Ice Creamery opened right across the street from Tabby's. New-Vel served different flavors like granola tutti-frutti and soybean swirl. They also had pistachio Popsicles.

"Look!" mewed an excited Tabby kitten. "They gave me a paper hat and a balloon—free!"

That very morning, Tabitha counted seventeen of Tabby's best customers going into New-Vel.

"Tom, we're just too old-fashioned," she said with a sigh.

"Nonsense," growled Tom. "We've got something that New-Vel can't give them— T.T.F.F. They'll be back begging for it, so you'd better start mixing."

Sadly Tabitha went into the kitchen to mix up a fresh batch, just in case. As she was reaching for a can of fudge syrup, she knocked over another can, and it fell on her head. Luckily she wasn't badly hurt, just shaken up.

But when she got out the mixing bowl, she
couldn't remember what to put in or how
much.

"Tom, I've forgotten the recipe!" she gasped.
"Just when we need it most."

"Lock the doors," said Tom. "Kittens, we've
got work to do."

And for a whole week Tom and his wife and the kittens mixed and stirred, stirred and mixed, trying to reinvent T.T.F.F. They even tried a pinch of fresh catnip.

"It's no use," said Tabitha, tasting the one hundred twenty-ninth sample. "There will never be any more T.T.F.F. at Tabby's."

"Then we'll close up for good," said Tom, switching off the blender as the kittens burst into tears. It was a sad day for the Tabby family.

"Oh, why didn't I write the recipe down!" wailed Tabitha as she flopped down in her favorite rocker. "Why was I so sure I'd always remember?"

She was so upset that she rocked over backward and fell out on the floor and bumped her head.

Tom and the kittens ran to help her up. Tom
gave her a glass of warm milk while the kittens
found her spectacles and tucked in her shawl.

Suddenly Tabitha jumped up. "It's come back to me!" she cried, hurrying to the mixing bowl. "Quick, Tom, write this down."

And while Tabitha mixed, Tom wrote down the recipe for T.T.F.F. Then he locked the valuable piece of paper in the safe. "There," said Tom, "T.T.F.F. will live forever."

When Tom opened the shop doors, a crowd
was waiting to come in. They were already
tired of New-Vel ice cream.

"T.T.F.F. is still the best ice cream in town!"
said one customer, ordering a sundae.

"And Tabby's is the only place to get it!" said another, dipping into his double dip.

"It sure beats paper hats and balloons," said another, sipping her soda.

All the Tabbys were as pleased as punch, especially Tabitha. She was so pleased that she shouted out, "Free ice cream for everyone!"